ANITA LOBEL

ALISON'S ZINNIA

Greenwillow Books, New York

Watercolor and gouache paints were used for the full-color art.
The type face is Fenice.

Printed in Singapore by Tien Wah Press
First Edition
1 2 3 4 5 6 7 8 9 10

Library of Congress Cataloging-in-Publication Data
Lobel, Anita.
Alison's zinnia / by Anita Lobel.
p.   cm.
Summary: Alison acquired an amaryllis for Beryl
who bought a begonia for Crystal—and so on through
the alphabet, as full-page illustrations are
presented of each flower.
ISBN 0-688-08865-1.
ISBN 0-688-08866-X (lib. bdg.)
[1. Flowers—Fiction. 2. Alphabet.]
I. Title. PZ7.L7794Al 1990
[E]—dc20 89-23700 CIP AC

FOR SWEET WILLIAM GILES, *CON AMORE*

Alison acquired an Amaryllis for Beryl.

A

Beryl bought a Begonia for Crystal.

Crystal cut a Chrysanthemum for Dawn.

C

Dawn dug a Daffodil for Emily.

D

Emily earned an Easter lily for Florence.

E

Florence found a Forget-me-not for Gloria.

F

Gloria grew a Gaillardia for Heather.

G

Heather hosed a Hyacinth for Irene.

H

Irene inked an Iris for Jane.

Jane jarred a Jack-in-the-pulpit for Kathleen.

J

Kathleen kept a Kalmia for Leslie.

K

Leslie left a Lady's slipper for Maryssa.

L

Maryssa misted a Magnolia for Nancy.

M

Nancy noticed a Narcissus for Olga.

N

Olga ordered an Orchid for Paulette.

O

Paulette plucked a Peony for Queenie.

P

Queenie quilted a Quaker-lady for Regina.

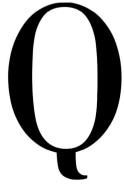

Regina raised a Rose for Susan.

R

Susan searched for a Sweet william for Tina.

S

Tina tended a Tulip for Ursula.

T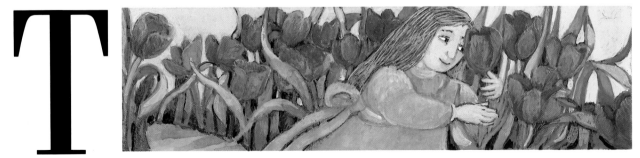

Ursula uprooted an Urtica for Virginia.

U

Virginia veiled a Violet for Wendy.

V

Wendy washed a Water lily for Xantippa.

W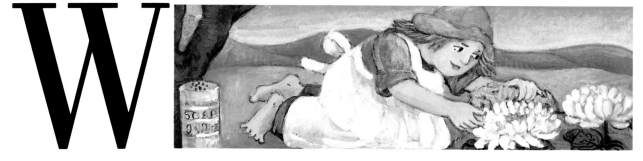

Xantippa x-ed a Xanthium for Yolanda.

X

Yolanda yanked a Yucca for Zena.

Y

Zena zeroed in on a Zinnia for Alison.

I love to draw and paint flowers. Ever since I illustrated *The Rose in My Garden*, I have mulled over the possibility of doing another picture book with flowers as the central theme.

Last summer, while visiting my friend Billy in Vero Beach, Florida, I rented a car. I had never been to Florida. I was thrilled by the driving, by the ocean, the open sky, and the quaint, manicured town that has streets named Azalea, Bougainvillea, Camelia, Dahlia, etc.—alphabetically!

One midday, after an exciting drive to Publix, I returned to find Billy arranging books in his library. He handed me *Pioneering with Wildflowers* by Senator George Aiken. Beryl Markham's biography, which we had just read, lay on the coffee table. We had also recently become acquainted with a British lady named Beryl.

The lushness of the alphabetic streets, the book on flowers, the name Beryl, all began to do a dance in my head. Could this be the idea I had been waiting for? An idea for a flower alphabet book? It took a bit of weeding before I found a way to connect flowers to girls' names. Once I found the verbs, it all seemed wickedly simple. Girl-verb-flower, linking fluidly and gracefully from page to page and connecting the last action in the book back to the beginning. I wrote it, A to Z, on the plane flight back to New York. The twenty-six flower paintings were not so simple. I worked on them for more than a year.

In selecting the flowers, I picked first those I really wanted to paint. But, of course, I had to bow to the needs of the alphabet. Some flowers behaved like divas, while others took direction very well. The chorus of little girls, without exception, behaved splendidly.

As a little girl in Poland, I remember weaving chains of flowers and wreaths for my hair. *Kwiatuszki*, the Polish word for "little flowers," is one of the special words remaining to me from the language I spoke as a child.

Anita Lobel
1989